W9-CLU-731

Baby Polar

by
Yannick Murphy

Houghton Mifflin Harcourt
Boston   New York

Illustrated by
Kristen Balouch

For my cubs,
Hank, Louisa, and Kit
—Y.M.

For Marley
—K.B.

Baby Polar stood between his mother's legs. He imagined she was a cave. Only the cave wasn't made of stone or rock, but of her thick fur and warm body. Baby Polar liked it there. He didn't feel the icy wind there. And he could hear the beating of his mother's heart.

"Look, a storm is coming,"
Mama Polar said.

Baby Polar saw dark clouds crossing over the blue sky.
Soon, flakes of snow began to fall.
Baby Polar wished he could go outside and play.

"Can I go play in the snow?" asked Baby Polar.
"Only for a little while. This might be a big storm,"
Mama Polar said.

Baby Polar walked out of his cave.
The snow was beautiful.

He held out his paw and watched
the pretty crystals melt on his black pad.

He turned his face up to the falling snow.

10

He held out his tongue and tasted the white flakes.

The snow started coming down hard.
It started to get deep.

So Baby Polar lay down in the snow,
with his round belly facing the sky.
He moved his furry legs up and down.
Swish, swish. He was making wings.

He stood up and saw the shape
he had made in the snow.

"Look at the Snow Goose I made,"
called Baby Polar to Mama Polar.

"Not now," Mama Polar said. "The storm is coming closer. It's time to come back."
"But I want to keep playing," Baby Polar said as he skated across the ice.

He looked behind him
at the trails he had made.

He made loop-de-loops.

He made crisscrosses.

He zigged and zagged.

Then Baby Polar noticed the sky had grown very dark.

He couldn't see his loop-de-loops or crisscrosses.
It was snowing so hard that he couldn't see
his own paw in front of him.

The wind was blowing so strong that it hurt his face.

He wished he were with his mother.
He wished he could feel her warm body
around him like a cave.

"Mama Polar, where are you?" he called.

But there was no answer,
only the howling of the cold wind.
Baby Polar started to cry.
His tears froze and stuck to his cheeks
like diamonds.

Baby Polar wanted to get out of the storm.
Great gusts of wind whipped through the air.

They blew falling flakes of snow from side to side and from here to there.

He kept walking.

He came to a white hill.
The hill was made of snow.
He dug into the snow.

He dug and dug, the white snow flying behind him.

He made a big hole in the hill and stood inside it. It was warm, like a cave. Baby Polar liked it there. He didn't feel the icy wind there. And he could hear the beating of his mother's heart.

Mama's heart!

Baby Polar jumped outside the cave
and poked at the hill.
"Mama Polar, is that you?" he said.
Then Mama Polar shook her fur coat
so that the snow fell off her.

"Yes, I'm Mama Polar. But who are you?" she said.
"Are you a little snowball that has rolled into me?"

"I'm not a snowball. I'm me. I'm your Baby Polar."

Baby Polar shook his fur coat so that the snow fell off
and Mama Polar could see him.

Mama Polar laughed and kissed the top of his head.
"Why, yes. You are my Baby Polar, aren't you?
But what are you doing standing out in the storm?
Come back inside and keep warm."

Now that he was with Mama Polar, the storm was beautiful to watch. He stood between his mother's legs and imagined she was a cave. Only the cave wasn't made of stone or rock, but of her thick fur and warm body. He didn't feel the icy wind there. And he could hear the beating of his mother's strong Polar heart.

BOBBY BEAR
AT THE FAIR

**Story and Illustrations
by Marilue**

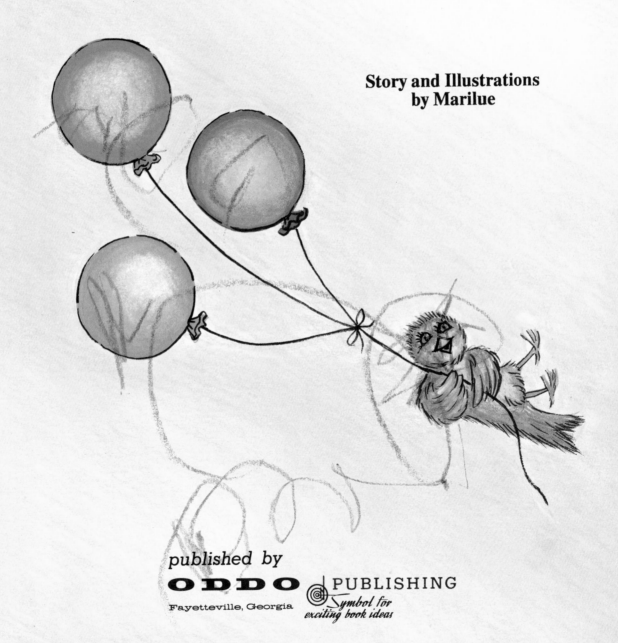

published by
ODDO PUBLISHING

Fayetteville, Georgia

*Symbol for
exciting book ideas*

Library of Congress Catalog Card Number 88-063232
ISBN 0-87783-250-1 (Library Binding)
ISBN 0-87783-237-4 (Paperback)

Printed in the United States of America

"Come with me!"
Said Bobby Bear.
"Let's go to
The big Fall Fair!

"Mother and Father
And Grandpa Bear
Said we will all
Enjoy a day there!"

4

"Will there be rides,"
Asked the bunny,
"And lots of games
That are funny?"

"Yes," said Bobby,
"The fair's a real treat
With rides and games
And good things to eat!

5

"Mother made jam
    And apple bread
    And chocolate chip
    Cookies, too!" he said.

6

"Go to your garden,"
Said Father Bear.
"Pick the biggest
Vegetables there.

"The biggest fruit
Or vegetable, too,
May win a special
Prize for you."

Bluebird chirped, "There's
So much to choose!
Bobby, I'm sure
You cannot lose!"

"Let's bring that pumpkin,"
Said Cousin Boo,
"That watermelon,
Squash and corn, too!"

"Fill the wagon!"
Said Bobby Bear.
"We might win a
Prize at the fair!"

Smiling and laughing
They walked along,
Singing a cheerful,
Happy "bear" song.

They pulled their goodies
Down the woodland trail,
Then over the hill
And across the vale.

"I see the fair!
Look everyone!
What shall we do
To start the fun?"

"Go play some games,"
Said Mother Bear.
"The Ring-Toss booth
Is over there."

Bunny asked his friends,
"Is that hard to do?"
"No. Just ring the bottle,"
Said Cousin Boo.

"Take a turn!
Toss a ring!
You might win
A Fuzzy Thing!"

"My toss won!"
Said Bunny, surprised.
"That Fuzzy Thing
Is now my prize!"

"Come, let's ride
The merry-go-round!
Up and down
And round and round."

"We are flying
In the air.
Hold the ropes!"
Said Bobby Bear.

15

"Candy apples!
Please, Mr. Goat,
Give us four with
An extra-thick coat!

16

"Mmmm! They're sticky
And very sweet.
Candy apples
Are a real treat!"

17

"See the ferris wheel!"
Said Father Bear.
"Would you like to take
A ride up there?"

Up and down
They circled around.
"I see the sky!"
"I see the ground!"

Bobby shouted,
"Hold on everyone!
This ferris wheel
Sure is fun!"

"Throw a ball!
Pop any balloon!
Win a toy!"
Said Mr. Raccoon.

"I see something
Blue and Pink.
It must taste good,
Don't you think?"

21

Mr. Goat smiled.
"It's cotton candy.
See the sugar
Spin so dandy?

"Here is one
For each of you,
Mother, Father,
And Grandpa, too."

23

"The roller coaster!"
    Exclaimed Mother Bear.
"I know you'll like that.
    You can get on there."

"It's so high,"
    The bunny cried,
"It looks like
    A big, long slide!"

"Don't be scared, Bunny.
Just hold on tight.
This ride's the most fun!
You'll be all right!"

"Ice cream! Cold ice cream!
Get yours now!
I have all flavors!"
Called Mrs. Cow.

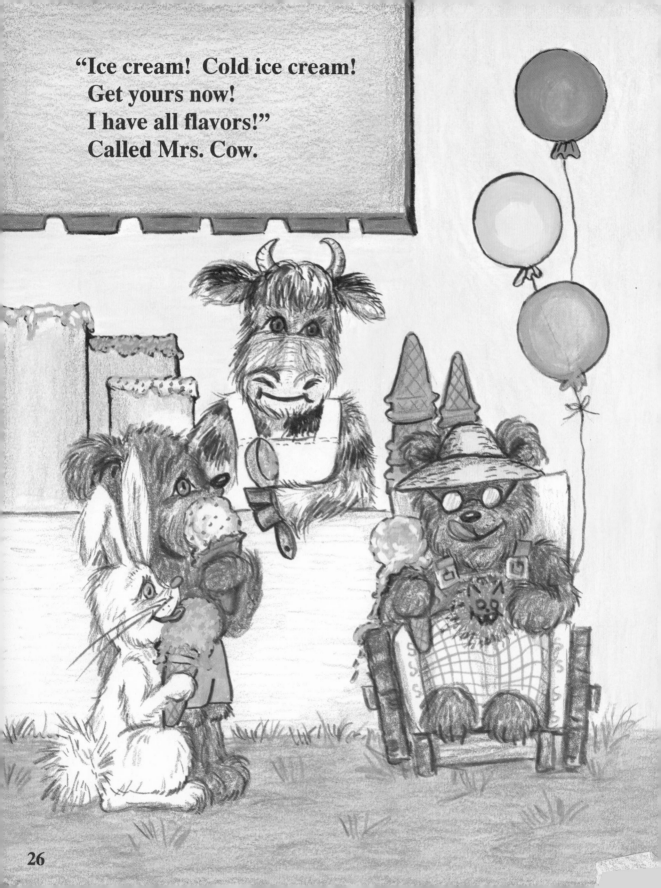

"Popcorn! Fresh popcorn!
 Buy a bag or box!
 I've caramel, too!"
Proclaimed Mr. Fox.

"I ate too much,"
  Moaned the bunny.
"I feel full and
  Kind of funny!"

"I feel dizzy,
  And funny, too,
From all the rides."
  Sighed Cousin Boo.

"I'm sure you'll feel better,"
Said Father Bear,
"When you see the surprise
That's over there!"

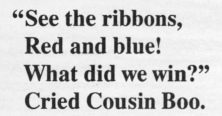

"See the ribbons,
Red and blue!
What did we win?"
Cried Cousin Boo.

"See that note, Bobby?
What does it say?
Please read it to us
Right away!"

" 'This is the big
Prize you have won —
More rides and treats
For everyone!' "

about the author and illustrator

MARILUE is the pen name of Marilue Johnson. A native of Grand Forks, North Dakota, Marilue began her art career at the Walker Art School in Minneapolis, Minnesota, and was awarded a scholarship in 1950. Her broad spectrum of accomplishments include teaching art, working for leading agencies in the Midwest, creating murals and commissioned paintings and sculptures, and art director for Univac Educational Division.

Her biography appears in *Outstanding Women of America, North Dakota Artists, Contemporary Authors,* and *International Authors and Writers Who's Who.*

As an honorary member of the International Platform Society, Marilue has given numerous book seminars at schools and various organizations. She has also made several guest appearances on television talk shows.

Her interest in painting, sculpture, and archaeology has been expanded by travels to Mexico, the Caribbean Islands, South America, Portugal, and Spain.

Marilue has illustrated 27 Oddo publications, nine of which she has also authored. A recent book she illustrated, *Bobby Bear and Uncle Sam's Riddle*, is the recipient of the George Washington Honor Medal awarded by the nationally recognized Freedoms Foundation at Valley Forge.

Marilue lives in Santa Fe, New Mexico, where she continues to paint and write Bobby Bear's endless adventures.